A GOOSEY FARM STORY

THE WISHING TOWER

Also published by Collins

A Goosey Farm Story: Dog's Journey *Gene Kemp*

A GOOSEY FARM STORY

THE WISHING TOWER

GENE KEMP

Illustrated by Paul Howard

Collins
An imprint of HarperCollinsPublishers

First published in Great Britain by Collins in 1998
Collins is an imprint of HarperCollins*Publishers* Ltd
77-85 Fulham Palace Road, Hammersmith,
London, W6 8JB

1 3 5 7 9 8 6 4 2

Text copyright © Gene Kemp 1998
Illustrations copyright © Paul Howard 1998

ISBN 0 00 675297 7

Printed and bound in Great Britain by
Caledonian International Book Manufacturing Ltd,
Glasgow G64

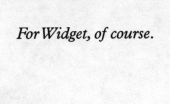

For Widget, of course.

Ancient
Monument

Stoney

PROLOGUE

It was dark in the wood. Tall trees towered over us shutting out the sky. Brambles snatched and scratched at our jeans, wrapping themselves around our legs as if they wanted us to stay there and be part of the wood and them. Frizzy, the little poodle, whimpered. Her woolly body was caught in a long snaking branch and she couldn't move. She squeaked at me desperately. Ahead of me Red Hanna, the whippety mongrel, forged up the path, her long nose pointing the way. At the sound of Frizzy's cries, she looked round, then ran back to her and pushed her with that nose, as if to say: Come on. Come on, then. Why are you hanging about? Let's get on. There might be *rabbits*!

"I thought you said this was a path, Widget," grumbled my brother Tim, as we pulled at the branches to free Frizzy. She squeaked a lot until Red Hanna licked her nose and then she quietened. At last we set her free, but at that moment a jagged flash of lightning shot down through the trees painting them purple, black, grey, outlining them in gold.

"We'll be struck!" yelled Tim. "I'm off home." And he belted back over the nettles, the brambles, the fallen branches and the dead leaves. The dogs, Hanna and Frizzy, shot after him. Any rabbits or other wild things there might be didn't matter any more. And if there was a mysterious Tower in the woods, who cared? Not me.

As lightning lit up the trees with its unearthly glow and thunder banged like a big bass drum we ran faster than we'd ever run before – Hanna way ahead – back along the not-much-of-a-path, through the gap to the track leading around the wood, over the gate to the fields, racing for the lane and home. Almost there and Sam Cat comes out, quite dry, from under a hedge, as the storm rolled away over the moor and all was quiet again except for us. Flinging ourselves into the kitchen – crash, bang, splash – home and safe, but not dry.

"Just drip by the door, will you?" cried Mum. "I'll get the towels. Don't shake water *everywhere*, Hanna. Glory, glory. You couldn't be wetter! What a storm! I'm glad you're back. I was just coming to meet you."

We stood there as she talked and little puddles formed all around us on the stone kitchen floor.

Chapter One

RAIN

I stood staring out of the window at the rain pouring down. It looked as if it was never, never, never going to stop. It had rained yesterday and the day before and the day before that and it would rain again tomorrow.

"I wish, I wish, I wish something *magic* would happen!" I'm always looking for magic, the surprise just around the corner (sending you round the bend, Dad said when I told him once), the view from the top of the hill, the wonderful thing that will happen next week.

I concentrated really hard, deep inside, squinting my eyes and clenching my fists.

Then I opened my eyes slowly. Perhaps Dad had come home on leave from the Navy early and was coming in NOW just like *that*.

I waited. Nothing.

Perhaps Mum would call out, "Guess what I've found in the cupboard. It must be left over from Christmas."

I waited. Nothing.

Perhaps she'd walk in waving an envelope and say, "I've just found this on the mat and it says we've won millions of pounds and we're going to sail around the world with Dad."

I waited. Nothing.

I looked around the room. Tim was playing with a football game and shouting, "Goal!" "Now!" "Brilliant!" Hanna, our red mongrel, lay stretched out watching, eyes half-closed. She knew better than to disturb him – Tim goes ballistic if his game gets messed up. Dizzy Frizzy, the white miniature poodle, lay in her basket curled around two white wuzzy balls; her puppies, Jazz and Pop.

"Come on, Widget," said Mum, who was

painting at the table, as she always does. "Don't just stand there looking miserable. Find something to do."

"What?"

"Play with one of *your* games."

"No!"

"Have a go on the computer."

"No."

"You haven't finished your jigsaw puzzle."

"It's too hard."

"Paint a picture."

"What? Of rain? *No*."

"Make something. Read a book. Write a letter. Write a story. Just don't stand there looking bored. The rain *will* stop."

"Suppose… suppose it rained for ever!"

"Then we'd build an ark. Like Noah. And all the animals could go in two by two…"

"But I want to do something *now*…"

"Well, I know what I'm going to do," Mum said. "I'm going to clear out that old chest in the attic. You can help me."

"Oh, I thought it would be something exciting…"

"Well, maybe it will. That old chest hasn't been touched since we moved here. Who knows what we'll find? Come on, stop moping about. Come and help."

"It'll be cold up there."

"Put another sweater on and stop being so *feeble*. When I was your age—"

"Oh, don't start that again. I'll come with you. And Hanna and Frizzy, you can come as well since you're not going for a walk in this downpour."

At the word 'walk' Red Hanna pricked up her ears, stuck out her long front paws and s-t-r-e-t-c-h-e-d slowly, yawning, just as Russet, her mother, used to do. Russet – the bestest of *all* the dogs we'd had – was run over last September and we missed her something rotten! Frizzy fretted so much that we sent her away to friends on the far side of the moor. But Frizzy missed *us* and in the worst Dartmoor blizzard for years she'd found her way back home across the snowbound moor. Of course she stayed here after that and settled in with Red Hanna, until her own puppies were born – those white balls of wool tucked up in the basket, snoozing. Very valuable, my mother told me, for Dizzy Frizzy, Jazz and Pop all had pedigrees as long as a High Street and their real names were very grand. Red Hanna wasn't very grand at all. No one could work out *her* pedigree.

"Oh, come on," my mother said. "Don't stand there daydreaming. Come and *do* something. Hanna's ready – she's wagging her tail. Come on!"

I followed her up the stairs and into the attic. It's always fairly dark up there, but it was really gloomy on this miserable day. Mum switched on the light. But the bulb didn't light up. "Dead as a doornail," she sighed. "Why 'dead as a doornail'?" I asked her. "Why isn't it dead as something else, like as dead as that horrible old spider I'm looking at?"

"Just stay there." She sounded snappy. "I'll go and get a new bulb and some candles. Don't mess about. Wait for me." Off she trotted downstairs, quite slowly because of the baby she was having.

The attic was full of beams and old furniture and dust. But Hanna pushed her nose into my hand and it was warm and wet and friendly. She licked me and then, wriggle, squiggle, push, shove, Frizzy joined us, trying to push her nose in and get Hanna out of the way. But Hanna was bigger and stronger and she couldn't.

The old chest stood under the little window. It was dusty, but even in the gloom you could see the carvings on it. I brushed it over with Hanna's wagging tail.

"It might as well come in useful," I whispered in her ear, which twitched with pleasure. When she's miserable her ears droop and hang down.

Mum was back with Tim in tow. Typical, he can't bear to miss a thing. Muttering and swearing a bit, Mum changed the bulb which was old and stiff. The new one didn't work either.

"Must be the socket," she said, stopping Tim having a go – he wouldn't have been any good. "It's no use, I shall have to have a proper sort out up here. It's just that I never seem to find the time."

"That's 'cos you're always painting."

"Well, it earns money."

"I'd rather have your paintings than a clean attic. Anyway, I like it like this."

"It's mysterious," Tim said.

"It doesn't matter that the light's not working," said Mum, "we've got lots of candles for times when the power goes off."

Mum had bought old saucers to stand the candles in and we lit about eight or nine so it looked really storybookish in the candlelight.

And who should be there but Sam Cat, stalking round us silently, tail aloft, looking like part of the story. He can't bear being left out any more than Tim can. Sometimes he follows us on walks, even though he's growing old now. He was once very fierce, a real Top Cat, Boss Cat, but then he had a fearful fight with a weasel in one of the barns. He killed it, but was very ill from the wounds and afterwards he was quieter and more gentle, but still our own Sam Cat.

"The chest's not dusty like everything else," Mum said as she lifted up the lid. Hanna wagged her tail but I didn't say anything. It was *our* secret.

As the lid went up and we looked inside by the shining light of the candles, I cried out, "There must be some magic here!"

"Well, let's see what treasure the chest holds then!" Mum laughed.

It was empty. Except for a bit of paper in the corner.

We all looked at one another. Sam Cat sat down and licked himself. Frizzy ran downstairs, deciding it was time she got back to her puppies. Hanna leapt into the chest, very pleased with herself, quite sure we'd really opened it up just for her.

Downstairs the telephone rang.

"It might be Dad," Mum said. "Look, it's almost dark. Blow out the candles, Widget. I don't think it's magic time today after all. Careful."

And away she went.

Tim and I got Hanna out of the chest and blew out the candles, taking it in turn. Then Sam Cat jumped in, so we fished him out too. I picked up the scrap of paper.

"I'll just look at it…"

"Is it interesting?" asked Tim. "A treasure map?"

"No, it's a bill. For timber, I think."

"Come and speak to Dad on the phone. Quickly!" Mum called.

We shot down the stairs, me still clutching the scrap of paper. I put it by the phone as I talked to Dad.

It definitely wasn't a day for magic. He said he was sorry but his leave had been put back a month. He'd write a long letter to make up for it. Not that it could. But it was nearly teatime now. And it was smashing grub.

"Know something," Mum said later. 'It's stopped raining."

Chapter Two

THE MAP

A week later Mum finished her paintings, packed them up and sent them off. They were the illustrations for a book of funny poems. We'd read them all and thought they were very good, though Tim said there weren't enough football ones.

"Well, you write some, then," Mum grinned. Then she said we'd got to help her clear up as everywhere was untidy.

"Bits of paper and old games all over the place," she grumbled. "And I'm getting too fat with this baby I'm having, to bend down properly."

Tim tried to slip away upstairs. Hanna hid under the old chair in the kitchen and Frizzy curled around her puppies, the perfect picture of a good mother who mustn't be disturbed, whatever happened.

"I don't want to clear up," I said.

"Right, that's fine. But there's no pocket money for you at the weekend then."

"It's not fair."

"It's perfectly fair. I didn't make all this mess. We all did. So we'll all help tidy up."

"Tim's gone upstairs."

"Well, fetch him down again."

"Mum says you'll have no pocket money if you don't come and help," I shouted at the top of my voice from the bottom of the stairs.

"Thank you," Mum said. "I'm now deaf for life. *Go and fetch him or—*"

She meant it. So I ran and fetched Tim and we started to clear up. Boring, boring boring.

"Most of it's yours, Tim."

"No it's not. This piece of paper here's

yours. Look, the one you found in the old chest. You left it by the phone." He peered at it. "That's funny. You said it was a bill, but it's not. It's a sort of drawing."

"Here, let me see."

"Don't snatch. You nearly tore it."

"No, I didn't."

"Don't take it away. I want to see it as well."

"Come on, then."

We sat down on the floor and looked at the crumpled piece of paper – only it wasn't paper, but some funny stuff. Mum would know what it is.

"It's parchment," she told us. "Why, this is an old map! Somebody's written out a bill on the back of it, but that's not important. It's this map that matters."

We all gathered round it kneeling on the floor, the clearing up and Mum being too fat to bend over all forgotten.

"I can't make sense of it," Tim muttered.

"That's 'cos you're stupid…"

"So are you stupid!"

"Be quiet," cried Mum. "Let's try and read it properly."

"Perhaps it's Treasure Island."

"No – it's not an island. I don't think so, anyway."

"It's a... a map of round here. Here. Where we live!"

"Is our farm on it?" I asked.

"Yes, yes," Mum almost shouted. "Look at these lovely little drawings. And here's Goosey Farm."

"Yes, and lots more. Look, there's our lane leading to the road where—"

"Where Russet was killed," Tim finished.

Worried, I looked at Mum. She'd cried for days about Russet, Hanna's mother, getting run over. She blamed it on herself because she'd let her off the lead in the road when she shouldn't have. I didn't want her to start crying again, but she said cheerily enough:

"Yes, but we won't think about that now. And we've got Hanna. She's just like Russet."

"And she's even more red-coloured."

"Let's find some more places. Look – there's the village and the church"

"Here's the river and the clapper bridge."

"What about the stone circle by the river?"

"Yes, it's here too."

"I've found Stoney Farm!" Peter and Christopher, our friends, live there.

"The old burial chamber's here. It's labelled 'Ancient Monument'."

Three granite slabs in a field with one laid on the top, looking rather like a mushroom, built 3,000 years ago by Neolithic ancestors. (And spooky. Very.)

"I like seeing Goosey Farm," Tim said, patting the place. "I'm glad we came here."

We'd left our little house in the city to come and live at Goosey Farm, with its two staircases and rooms that go on forever, and the fields and moors of Devon all around us. And now it felt as if we'd never lived anywhere else and the people round here didn't call us 'Grockles' (tourists) any more.

"Look, look!" I cried. "In this old wood – Rushford, I think it's called – not far from here if you go across the fields. Look!"

"Oh, yes – there's a little tower in the wood!" cried Mum.

And then I knew. Magic had arrived that rainy day when I'd wished for it. The Tower would be magic. I just knew.

"Mum, Tim, we've got to find that Tower!"

Chapter Three

THE FIRST ATTEMPT

We found the Tower in the wood, but not the first time we searched for it.

We set off armed with the old map, Tim and me, Hanna and Frizzy. Mum couldn't come as some people were coming to see her. She wasn't very keen on us going by ourselves.

"Be careful," she warned. "I don't know if you should really go on your own..."

"We'll be OK. It's not far away."

"All the same – take care."

We went down our lane, then followed a path going through several fields. The wood loomed ahead of us, set on a hill, so all the trees growing on it rose into a big mound against the sky. Even further away was a faint purple smudge in the distance – the moor. Everything was still and quiet in the early morning; no noise anywhere as yet. Even the dogs walked along quietly.

We climbed over the gate from the fields onto a rough track that ran beside a hedge circling the wood. Below us in the sloping fields lay a farm so old it looked as if it had grown there – Goosey Farm.

"Somewhere in these woods is the Tower," I whispered as we walked along the path, the moss silencing our footsteps.

"Yeah, but where do we get in?" Tim whispered back.

It was a whispery sort of place. Not a sound. Not a murmur. Overhead a buzzard hawk hovered in the sky, blue when we started out, but now getting covered with grey and purple storm clouds.

The trees loomed above us, branches bare for it was early spring. Inside would be the Tower and magic, but between us was a thick hedge of hawthorn and holly and brambles. Plus a few nettles to make it really cosy.

"Let's try further on."

We ran on, making our way along the track outside the wood, but still the hedge was high and thick between us and the wood.

"Perhaps we'll find a gap." I said.

"No chance," said Tim.

There didn't seem to be a way in as we ran along. But just when we had almost given up hope we found a gap beside a tree and we pushed through it into the wood at last.

"I think there's a path here, Tim."

"It's not much of one. Ouch, that got me!" The long thorny arms of a bramble twisted around his legs.

"I don't like it, Widget."

"Shut up."

We went on with Frizzy and Hanna, finding our way through head-high plants and bushes, nettles and brambles. Twigs snapped under our feet. Ancient crooked trees grew all around – others towered high above us. Broken branches tripped us up.

By now the sky was almost black. A cold wind whistled up from nowhere and a thunderclap echoed in the distance... and that's where this story started.

"Did you find the tower?' asked Mum when we were safe at home, eating.

"There isn't any tower," Tim answered, his mouth full of food.

"Yes, there is. I know there is. But, Mum—"

"But what? Go on, Widget."

"I don't think it wants to be visited."

"Maybe I'd better come with you next time," Mum said. "Before I get too fat with this baby I'm having."

"Will you? Honest?"

"Yes. We'll find that tower yet!"

Chapter Four

THE SECOND ATTEMPT

A week later I wanted to go tower-hunting again.

"No," Tim said. "We shan't find that tower even if there is one. You can't see it in the wood from outside, can you? Well, if it was there you'd be able to see it, wouldn't you? And even if there ever was one I expect it's fallen down by now. If it's old like you say."

"Well, can we just try. Please. I'll give you half my pocket money on Saturday."

"Promise. Cross your heart and hope to die?"

"Promise. Cross my heart and hope to live for ever."

Mum accompanied us as we set off again with the dogs into the fields leading to the track. A few black and white cows stared at us as we made our way along, then just carried on grazing. All was quiet until – SPLAT – and all the cows looked up at us, as a great big ugly dog, with a smooth white face, red eyes, a black furry body and a plumy, swinging tail, landed among us, leaping up and greeting us like crazy.

Death's-head had arrived.

We call him Death's-head (though his real name's Spot and he belongs to a farmer neighbour) because if you meet him in the dark you can only see his white face and red eyes looking like a skeleton and it's scary. But he's as soppy as anything and loves us madly and gets out to come with us whenever he can. Most of all he loved Russet, and he fretted a long time when she was run over, but now he loves Hanna (who is very probably his daughter) nearly as much.

"Down, down, Death's-head!" we yelled, as he tried to knock us over so he could lick us properly, and we hurried on along the path before the cows came over. Cows didn't like him and always chased him off when they saw him.

"William the Conqueror listed Goosey Farm in his Domesday Book," Mum said softly, when she looked back at it. "A thousand years old – well nearly."

She was talking softly because the path, the wood and the farm gave out this atmosphere of knowing a secret, hiding something that it would tell you about in time, when it wanted to, but you must be careful not to trespass too far or it would be very frightening.

We followed the same way, along the same track with the same horrible hedge. But it was warmer this time and the spring flowers were coming out; the primroses, the celandines, even some violets, and the trees were getting their leaves, colouring them green.

But it was still very quiet and the hedge was as thorny and unfriendly as ever as we reached the gap by the tree.

"I'm not going that way again," said Tim. "Let's find another gap."

"Suppose there isn't one." I replied.

However, a few yards further on we found a space a bit larger than the first one. The dogs rushed through first followed by Tim and me, Mum bringing up the rear more slowly. At first it was fairly easy going but then it suddenly got worse. We struggled a bit, not talking at all. Somehow you didn't want to speak loudly. There was a feeling that someone, *something* might be watching and listening, a feeling that you shouldn't be there. I picked up Frizzy. Red Hanna and Death's-head leapt and jumped their way over broken branches and strange plants. Twigs snapped under our feet like guns going off. Ancient crooked trees grew all around us. We had to push past branches hanging over the path.

A fallen tree lay with broken branches like a defeated dead dragon. I tripped over another that reached out like a crab's claw.

"These trees are furry…" Tim said, pushing away a branch.

"It's lichen, stupid…"

"*I'm* not stupid. *You're* stupid, bringing us here. We're probably in danger like they tell us all the time. We'll be found dead and it'll be all your fault."

"It's a fairy tale. Like the woods and roses in *Sleeping Beauty* grew up all around the castle."

"I'd rather have a football," Tim answered. "I don't like fairy tales much, Widget, and I want to go home."

"I think that might be a good idea. I'm not sure this is the right way," said Mum, who had paused for a moment, for she'd got a stitch.

The wood changed. The path dwindled away and there ahead of us was a high wall of holly bushes. Red Hanna turned her long nose to me, her beautiful eyes full of – what?

Frizzy whimpered, hiding her face under my arm. Death's-head ran up and down trying to find a place to get through. He's got a thicker coat that the rest of us.

"I can't go through those prickles. You can't want us to go through all that lot, Widget. Even *you* aren't that crazy."

"Tim, Mum – please. Let's try to find a way through."

"No," said Tim.

"Let's leave it," said Mum. "I think we ought to be getting back."

Then Death's-head howled. He does that sometimes and it's dreadful. The wood echoed with the miserable, horrible, terrible sound of Death's-head howling – one of the worst noises I know.

We bolted. Faster than the time before. Even Mum wasn't hanging about.

But then, to relieve my disappointment, Dad came home on leave with lots of presents that he calls rabbits, and Aunt Dinah came for the weekend bringing her boyfriend, Fred. And Granny and Grandad turned up, so we had a party and a great time and I forgot about the Tower, for part of me didn't want to think too much about it because it scared me, though I wouldn't say so to Tim.

After everyone had gone it was quiet again. Tim went off to play with Chris and Peter Stone at the next farm and I lay on my bed and read, with Hanna and Frizzy helping. After a while I thought about the Tower and the longing to find it came over me once more. I ran downstairs to ask Mum if we could go again, but she was talking to Chris and Peter's mother. Besides, I thought to myself, she looks as if she's getting too fat to manage it now. I joined Sam Cat in the farmyard where he was fast asleep.

A shadow fell over me – much too big for Tim. I looked up and saw John Ellis, a very large and powerful, but quiet boy, who lived on a farm on the High Moor. He'd ridden over on his pony with Baggins, Hanna's brother. Baggins had been the ugliest of the litter where Hanna was the prettiest. Baggins and Hanna sniffed noses and bottoms and wagged tails furiously. Both the dogs played around, excited by Baggins and the pony. Sam Cat stalked off in disgust, nose in the air. And

I found myself telling John Ellis all about the Tower. He knows everything about the countryside around here and about Dartmoor, so he'd be sure to tell me about it.

"Yup, I know it," he said slowly, at last, when I'd finished talking. He never hurried. "Rushford wood is very old, you know. Goes right back to Domesday time."

"And the Tower?" I asked.

"No, that ain't that old. They built that as a watchtower – maybe to look for the Frenchies if Napoleon invaded us. I once went there with my dad."

"Will you take *us* there? We can't find the way."

"Yup. Bring some sandwiches and some little coins and I'll come and take you up next Saturday. Bye now."

And he was off on his pony, Baggins running alongside. Hanna wanted to go with them. I had to hold her back.

John turned around and lifted his hand to me. "They call it the Wishing Tower!" he cried, and was gone.

Chapter Five

THIRD TIME LUCKY!

John came for us just as he'd said he would, leaving his pony at Goosey Farm. Death's-head also arrived early as if he'd known all about the expedition. Mum had done a packed lunch and Tim said he didn't mind going with John Ellis.

"I'll feel safe with him," he muttered. "He's not nutty like you, Widget."

I pulled a face at him. "Thank you very much! All the times I've looked after *you*. Shan't bother in future."

We'd got two silver five pence coins each,

not that I'd a clue why we were supposed to bring them, for there weren't any shops on the way. We got away early before Chris and Peter found out and wanted to join us, for we wanted to be on our own. At least I did. I liked them but there wouldn't be any magic if they were around shouting and arguing and scrapping.

We followed the same path through the fields and from the track I could see Goosey Farm, crouched down low like an old farm animal. John Ellis loped ahead of us on his long legs. Hanna, Baggins, Frizzy and Death's-head ran along, as good as gold with John. We went past the first two openings this time, and continued along the track as it curved around the wood. It was quiet early morning. A buzzard hawk circled above. Same one, I thought. Must live here. But the air was warm and the spring flowers were opening everywhere: primroses, celandines, wind-flowers and violets. The trees and bushes were leafy now.

We ran steadily on. Then John stopped quite suddenly, just like that.

"We're here," he said.

Of course it was the place. There were two tall, old, grey granite pillars on each side of a gap in the hedge and a clear path wound ahead of us through the bluebell leaves, soft and shining. All the bushes and small trees grew on the sides of the path, leaving it easy and open, and there wasn't a bramble or nettle in sight. Nothing scratchy. Nothing to hold on to you and tear or sting.

A huge branch, with what looked like a broken arm and hand, pointed to where we should go like a signpost. The dogs' tails wagged as we climbed steadily upwards. There were lots of trees but none to stop us. Nothing getting in our way. I thought I could see the holly-tree hedge but it was far off to the right.

The hill was flattening out now. We must be nearly at the top. A turn in the path took us through and behind more trees. I was breathless. I knew the Tower was there. I'd see it any minute now. And a space opened out, silver birch trees shining all around and other trees I didn't know. Beautiful trees all in a circle round the hill. John Ellis grinned at me.

A lawn of blue-green grass lay in the middle of the trees and there were bushes covered in white blossom. On the other side of the lawn stood the tower, *my* Tower, a very little grey stone tower. It had an arched window and three slitted windows and battlements. Grey stones lay round it where some battlements had toppled to the ground. Behind the tower dark fir trees loomed, taller than it was.

An archway looked at us, inviting *us* to look. Its door stood open. We ran towards it, then stopped. I'd thought so much about it that now I was nearly there I was almost afraid to go in. Then we walked through the door.

Chapter Six

At Last

Up and up we climbed, round and round. The stairs were narrow and crumbling with broken bits of rock scattered all over them. I could feel the walls as I went up. They were gritty and damp. The dogs pushed past us pointing long noses. I reached the top in no time at all as it was such a tiny tower and came out on to a landing where we could see over the battlements to the treetops and the birds flying in the sky. There was the moor in the distance and somewhere, the sea.

"We're on top of the world!"

"But what's it for?" cried Tim.

"It's a look-out tower," John told him. "In case the enemies come."

"You mean... Hitler?"

"Yup, and before him, Napoleon and the Frenchies."

"Who was Napoleon?"

"He wanted to invade us. Like Hitler."

"But he didn't, did he?"

"No."

"And now they're both dead, but the Tower's still here. Funny," I said.

"If anybody came now, I'd shoot them from here, *bang, bang* – they're dead!" Tim cried.

"What with?" I asked him.

"Bows and arrows, like in *Robin Hood*. Or pour boiling water over them. Or chuck stones at them."

"I'd rather have a tournament down there on the green lawn with knights in armour fighting for ladies in their beautiful gowns," I said.

"That's soppy."

"No, it's not. You've got no imagination, Tim. You only think about bashing things or playing football."

"Yeah, that's it. Let's go and play on the lawn, John," Tim cried. "I've brought my ball especially."

"No, let's explore the Tower first – else we might as well be back home," I cried, fed up.

So we went back down the stairs and into the two downstairs rooms, which were full of bits of rock and dark in the corners. An old mattress and some rags and bottles were heaped up in one corner.

"Some old tramp has slept here," John said, as the dogs sniffed around the heap. Very smelly.

"It's not very magical," I said sadly.

"Come on, Widget. Let's eat our food on the lawn outside. It's warmer there."

So we sat in the bright sunshine and ate our food. It was warm and peaceful.

"It's a silly tower," Tim said. "It's too little to be any good for anything."

Tim made me mad at times.

"It's big like the Tardis in *Doctor Who*. Bigger than it seems to be. You said, John – you said it was called the Wishing Tower."

"Yup, that's right."

I waited, but he just went on chewing.

"Well, tell me. There's got to be a *reason*."

"I'm no good at tellin' stories."

"Oh, please try. Please, John. Then I can have a wish here."

"You'll 'ave to leave the last sarnie then.

An 'ave you got a silver coin?"

"Yes. Why?"

"You need one for the wishing."

"Why, what have I got to do? *Tell* me. And what's the story, anyway."

"I told you, I'm no storyteller."

"Try. *Please*. Then we can all have a wish."

"Can't we just play football instead?" Tim put in. "Unless it's a story about aliens."

"When we've heard the story and wished. Don't take that last sarnie. We've got to keep it!"

"OK, bossy cat. Let's get on with it."

We settled back on the grass. After a bit John began. "There was this girl, see, with a funny name."

"What?"

"Nest."

Tim rolled over and over, laughing fit to burst. Birds flew away out of the trees.

"Shut up. You're upsetting the Tower," I hissed at him.

"It was a Welsh name, I think. And she was rich. Very rich."

"Was she a Princess?"

"No, but she *was* a Lady, I think."

Tim groaned.

"If you don't shut up, I'll wish that something really, really horrible happens to you!!!" I yelled at him.

"I'll shut up," he said.

"Well, she lived in a grand 'ouse and 'ad all the fiddle-faddles – you know."

"Go on."

"Well, when she was just seventeen she went to Tavistock Fair with her cousin, and there she fell in love with a tinker who was selling pots and pans."

"Whatever for?" asked Tim.

"To cook with, of course."

"No, I meant what did she fall in love with a tinker for? I mean, it's not like a footballer or a pop star, is it, a tinker, I mean..."

"Oh, shut up. Go on, John."

"She said she wanted to marry 'im and 'er dad was right mad and locked 'er up in 'er room."

"Poor thing."

"Well, she climbed out of the window and rode away with the tinker on a 'orse and got lost until, at last, late at night they came to this tower and sheltered in it."

"Was there a storm, then?" I asked. "Oh, how could her father be so cruel?"

"I 'spect 'e didn't want 'er selling pots and pans, y'know, Widget. She wouldn't be any good at it, I don't reckon."

"Oh, go on with the story."

"The father followed 'er all the way from Wales with 'is men and everything, and they surrounded the tower."

"What happened then?"

"Well, Nest and – I don't know 'is name…"

"Oh, call him… I know, Tarquin."

"Fred's a better name," said Tim.

"Well, Nest and whoever it was looked out over the battlements and saw—"

"Dad and his Merry Men!" Tim cried.

"And all the 'orses and 'ounds and knew they couldn't get away…"

"How awful!"

"And 'er dad was shaking 'is fist and yelling and the 'ounds were belling…"

"Belling?"

"Oh, that's the noise they make. And 'er dad was telling 'er to come down and be a good girl or 'e'd put Fred…"

"Tarquin, you mean."

"In prison for kidnapping."

"Oh, how cruel!"

"So Nest cried, 'Someone, help please!' and knelt down and prayed."

"What did she pray?"

"That 'er dad would let 'em get married, of course. Then a voice said in 'er 'ead, 'Throw a silver coin over the parapet and a piece of the bread you have left (she'd brought some food with 'er) and wish – then see what 'appens'. And she did."

"And what *did* happen?"

"A stranger on 'orseback appeared, rode up to 'er dad and whispered in 'is ear. When 'e 'eard what 'e 'ad to say, 'er dad called up to Nest and the tinker and said, 'Dearest child, you shall marry the one you love, I promise on my honour'."

"Oh, how lovely."

"And a whole lot more men came and they all went back 'ome and Nest and…"

"Tarquin?"

"Fred?"

"…were married and they all lived 'appily ever after."

"Oh, how wonderful! So the Wishing Tower made Nest's dad change his mind and he let her marry a tinker."

"Yup, in a way, Widget, but it was the stranger speaking to 'im that really changed 'er dad's mind."

"What did he say, then? Tell me…"

"That stranger said, ''Old on. That tinker there is really Lord…'"

"Tarquin?"

"Fred?"

"'…of the Marches and is three times as rich as you are'. Lord Tarquin was playing the tinker for a bet."

I felt very let down by this.

"You mean the Tower isn't really a Wishing Tower? It didn't make the dream come true?"

"Yes, it does, but the wishes comes true in an ordinary way."

"Oh."

"It's better than nothing!"

"I'm going to have my wish then. I wish—"

"You mustn't tell anybody or it won't come true."

"Oh."

"I wish," shouted Tim, "that we could play with my ball. Now!" and he put his five pence and half the sarnie just inside the door.

"That won't come true because you said it out loud!"

"But it is coming true, 'cos I'm kicking the ball to John *now!*" And laughing all over his face, Tim kicked it high up in the air.

"See, Widget!"

But the ball flew higher and higher up over the Tower and into the crowded trees and bushes behind it. And though we searched and searched we couldn't find it.

Chapter Seven

DOWN TO EARTH WITH A BUMP

I went over and over the story of Lady Nest and the tinker in my mind. I pictured her on the Tower and her father with all his men gathered down below awaiting his orders and then the strange man riding up to her father and whispering in his ear, telling him that the tinker on the tower with his daughter Nest was really Lord Tarquin of the Marches, so she could marry her true love. I was just getting round to designing her wedding dress and thinking that I'd do a book on all the costumes...

"You're quiet," said my mother. "Hope

you're not sickening for something."

"Nah, she's just sickening," Tim put in, then went on with his football game, shouting, "Arsenal 8, Man United 8."

"That's not funny," I answered back, "and if you really want to know I was practising tables in my head. You have to be good at mental arithmetic these days."

"Good girl," Mum nodded at this feeble little porky, but I didn't want to tell her – not even my mother – about the Tower, Lady Nest, the tinker, knights of old, enchantment, maidens rescued from perilous dungeons, dragons, magicians – especially Merlin – spells, ogres, three-headed giants, quests, wonders, ancient stones with strange writing on them – brilliant, fabulous, fantastic, wicked, out-of-this-world happenings. Who wanted the ordinary world of tables, spelling, school, football, rounders, tidying up? Not me. My heart was in the Tower. There was my magic, wonderful world.

What would make it even more brilliant was if the wish I'd wished there in the doorway came true. I hadn't told anyone about it and I was keeping my fingers crossed. It was just a little humble wish to see if wishes made at the Tower really did come *true*. I mean, who cared if I didn't beat Caroline Mortimer at Spelling last week – it was just that we always got the same and it would be fun to do better for once. We always did the spelling tests on Friday and had the results on Monday. So there I was waiting to see. Could the Tower Magic work on the result? Would my wish come true? And in a perfectly ordinary way. No one would know. 'Cept me.

But at school on Monday we were told that our teacher, Mrs Cotter, wasn't very well and wouldn't be coming in. Caroline was also away. This rocked me a bit, but I thought it would be OK really. This tower, *my Tower*, had its own way of granting wishes – I hoped.

We'd got a supply teacher called Mrs

Biddulph. "Maths is my favourite subject," she called out, her voice going up and down as if she was singing. "And we're going to do lots of Maths and give Mrs Cotter a lovely surprise when she comes back at how very clever you all are. So we're going to do lots of lovely, lovely tables practice till you know them all in your heads! Come along, children dears! Robert, you start with your two times table. Shout it out just for us!"

TIMES
TABLES

"Can I use my calculator, Miss?" asked Robert.

"No, dear, you can do it all in your head. Come along, we'll all do it in our heads. We're going to do lots and lots of mental arithmetic. It'll be ever such *fun!*"

"I'd rather have a go on the computer," Robert answered, but Mrs Biddulph took no notice and soon we were all chanting tables and working out sums in our heads.

"That's it. Back to basics! That's what makes clever little girls and boys."

I tried to keep my mind on it all, but I was picturing Lady Nest in a wedding gown with a wreath of flowers on her flowing golden hair. Six maidens in rainbow-coloured silken gowns attended her, and somehow Merlin, the greatest of all magicians, was there, wearing a tall, pointed hat and a dark cloak covered in gold and silver – sun, moon and stars.

"Wake up! Wake up, child! Didn't you hear my question? Just answer it and stop daydreaming!"

I couldn't answer the question as I hadn't a clue what it was. Face getting redder and redder, I sat with my mouth open, Lady Nest and the Tower quickly disappearing far far away. "Help me!" I cried in my mind, desperately, frantically. "*Please!*"

Big John drawled the answer lazily from the back of the class – we were all in together, his class and mine, as a whole lot of children were away and so was another teacher as well as Mrs Cotter.

"I've been meaning to ask about this problem, Mrs Biddulph," he went on, capturing her attention, "can you explain this for me? I got it wrong last week and maybe you could help me with it."

"Yes, yes," she cried, "of course. The rest of you get out your books now and get on with your work."

I was saved.

In the shuffle and sort out no one noticed my red face hiding itself in my Maths book. Maybe, maybe, the Tower and school didn't mix. Maybe, maybe I'd better concentrate. I didn't like Mrs Biddulph. I don't think she cared much for me either.

Two things. One, I'd been paid out for my porky to Mum and two, Big John had saved me from trouble. And had I wished for the Tower to save me? I couldn't remember, really I couldn't.

Chapter Eight

THE MEASLE BUG

Ten of us ran through the woods along by the river.

"Now don't you go too fast, children, mind. Wait for me! I told you to go slowly, boys and girls, and then wait for me. Careful now. I don't want any of you to fall in now, or I shall get it in the neck, by golly. John, John, you slow down, then the others will! Wait! Wait! Be good children now."

Mrs Biddulph, who was a bit fat and wearing high heels, ran after us waving her arms and calling. But we were wild – being out in the woods on a fantastic spring day, with the sun shining through the trees, when normally we'd be in school doing, well, Maths, Science, Spelling. To be outside jumping over rocks with the trees all around us and hearing the River Teign sing its roaring song rushing over boulders and weirs down to the sea was magic.

I sang a song, happily, over the sound of the water. John was up in front, the Stone boys behind, then Ken, Tammy, Bridget, me, Mike, Patrick and Damien – out of school, but in school.

"We're going to the zoo," sang Patrick from the rear just ahead of Mrs Biddulph.

"No, we're on a Nature walk," I sang back.

"We're the Specials, the Champions…" bellowed Damien.

And we were. For we were the ones *who hadn't caught measles*. All the rest had gone down like skittles in a bowling alley. Caroline Mortimer and Mrs Cotter were the first with it and then one by one, next two by two, and finally three by three, the rest of the school followed. Tim went down with most of his class, but not me, nor the ten of us left with Mrs Biddulph.

We were having a great time. Art and Stories, Drama, Music, Dancing, Soccer, as well as the yes, yes, yes, of course, Maths, Science, Spelling. We all liked Mrs Biddulph now, even me. She brought in little prezzies for good work, she read us funny stories and we made a puppet theatre with Dracula the vampire, the chief character, made by Damien.

"Suits 'im. Typecasting," grinned John Ellis, for Damien has two fangy teeth at the side of his mouth and is a bit witchy looking.

Tim was at home being nursed by Mum. Hot, feverish and spotty, and angry because the days went by and I didn't catch the measle bug. He wanted me at home with him. But not me. None of us had caught it.

"We're the Specials. We're the Champions," Damien gloated again, sitting on a wall.

And being special we had special things to do – working out on all the gym apparatus, playing *all* the musical instruments, using lots of art stuff from the stock cupboard.

"What a horrible racket," cried Mrs Biddulph and set us off writing spooky music for the vampire play that we were going to perform for Mrs Cotter and all the measle bugs when they came back.

"I hope they never come back," said Chris Stone. "It's brill at school like this." He kicked a football around the playground. Bridget and Tammy were doing handstands against the wall. We all wore what we liked and the girls were in jeans.

"It's like we're out of time," I said.

"What d'you mean?" Chris Stone put in.

"Oh, we're in a time slip that's not ordinary time and when the others come back, time will start up again…"

"Her's nutty," said Ken, grinning. "The Widget's nutty. Allus was and allus will be."

I went for him and we had a scrap till John Ellis stopped it.

"You're his pet," Tammy whispered in my ear.

"Dunno what you mean," I muttered, going red, and I walked off indoors so I could get on with my painting which was, *of course*, of the Tower in the woods, with Lady Nest and Tarquin on the battlements, and her father and his Merry Men on the green grass down below. It was pretty hard to do but I liked it.

I wrote a poem to go with it:

O tower grey!
O tower high!
With battlements
Against the sky.

Great lords once had
Their days in you.
Kings visiting
Held court in you.

Suffering slaves
In a mouldy cell
Found your dark walls
A fearful hell.

But a maiden ran
Her knight to greet
And found all Heaven
Beneath her feet.

Banquets huge
Tournaments proud
And brave knights battling
Before a glittering crowd.

But now you stand
Old, cold and grey
And grass grows where
Lords ruled yesterday.

"Good, my dear," cried Mrs Biddulph. "Much better than your Maths!" She put a gold star on it and I was pleased, but then I thought I shouldn't have written it, and perhaps the Tower wouldn't like it. After all it was a secret, hidden tower and *my* friend, and now I'd given it away to everyone, especially when Damien said:

"Why hasn't it got a vampire in it? A tower's no good without vampires."

And he went to draw one but I stopped him, and then Mrs Biddulph cried out, "Wellingtons and anoraks, children! We're off for a Nature walk through the woods!"

She was so busy getting us ready she forgot to change her own shoes and that's why we were running ahead of her along by the River Teign.

Chapter Nine

NATURE WALK

Well, it wasn't really a Nature walk, more like a Nature run, but at last we calmed down, mainly because we were out of breath and had got stitches, some of us anyway.

"That's better," panted Mrs Biddulph. "Now I can tell you the names of the trees and the plants. Look, children, at that huge oak tree there…"

"No, Miss," John said politely. "That's not an oak tree, it's an ash. You can see its leaves aren't out yet, a good thing."

"Why is it a good thing?" asked Mrs

Biddulph, puzzled.

"Well, you see that other tree over there..."

We all looked where he pointed to a really wide, massive tree standing alone. It had all its leaves already.

"Now, that's an oak with all its leaves. You see, Miss, the farmers say:

If the ash comes out before the oak,
All the summer we have a soak.
If the oak comes out before the ash,
Fills the farmer's pockets with cash.

So as the oak tree's out first, we should 'ave a good summer."

We stared at him, gobsmacked.

"Thought you said you weren't good at telling things," I said.

He grinned. "Depends."

"My dad's pockets aren't full of cash," Chris Stone said. "He says we may have to sell Stoney Farm. It's hard for farmers, these days."

"I'm sorry," Mrs Biddulph said, then, "Look, children at those lovely white violets!"

"Sorry, Miss, they're windflowers, not violets," John sighed. "Sorry."

"I think this had better be *your* lesson," Mrs Biddulph said sadly. "I'm not much good at Nature, really."

"City people aren't," Chris Stone said.

She brightened up. "Well, maybe we'll spot some lovely little animals, children!"

"They won't come out with all the row we're making. They'll all be in their 'iding places."

"Yes, of course. Tell me, John, what's that bird up there?"

"That's a buzzard 'awk."

"I didn't think we got those in England now."

"Well, we do and it's 'unting."

Mrs Biddulph, who seemed to have forgotten all about basics, and was really very nice, brought out some Refreshers for us all.

"Hope the Inspectors don't find us chewing these in the middle of a wood," she laughed.

"Never mind, Miss, we shan't tell."

"No, don't, or I shall be for it. This is a Spelling lesson."

"I can spell 'nut'," Damien cried. "N-I-T."

We all fell about laughing, and Bridget asked, "Can we have a game of Hide and Seek?"

So we did. Over the rocks, behind the trees and the bushes we ran, and scrambled and hid until at last...

"Can we stop now, please."

Red, sweaty and happy, we got together and flopped on the ground.

"Thank you for *not* falling in the river or getting lost," Mrs Biddulph panted, beetroot-coloured.

"You're nice, so we didn't." Ken said, so she went even more beetroot coloured, then she looked at her watch.

"Time to go back or we'll all be for the chop!"

We'd turned to go back through the woods when Bridget said suddenly, "Couldn't we just go and see that tower of Widget's? She said its battlements go up to the sky so we ought to be able to find it. Please, Mrs Biddulph."

"Oh, no!" I cried before I could stop myself. "It's secret."

"Don't be mean," Bridget said. "It's not yours, is it? You don't own it. We've got more right to it than you because *we've* always lived here. *Come on*, you've got to show us where it is, Widget!"

I could feel the tears stinging behind my eyes. Why had I ever mentioned the Tower? I wished I'd never said anything about it. We couldn't all go trampling round it. It would ruin it. What could I say?

"Oh, it's too far away from 'ere," John said lazily. "About two to three miles. You'd never manage the walk, Bridget."

Mrs Biddulph chimed in, "Yes, we must hurry. We've only a quarter of an hour to get back to school and we've come quite a long way already. Right, off we go. I expect you can visit the tower another day, Bridget."

"Not if I can help it," I muttered under my breath as we struggled back, tired now and a bit cross because it was uphill all the way.

Chapter Ten

NOT MUCH FUN

Tim was getting better. Children were coming back to school, Caroline the first. Mrs Cotter took longer to come back as grown-ups always get things like measles and mumps worse than kids do, the doctor said, and so were slower getting better. When she did return I found out that I had come top in Spelling.

It didn't seem important but it made me sure that wishes made in the Tower did work.

And that made me want to visit it again and wish for Dad to come home, as he seemed to have been gone for absolutely ages and I longed to see him again. But Tim was grizzly, said he felt weak – much too tired to trek to the tower, which was rubbish anyway. Mum said I couldn't go on my own and there was too much work to do at Goosey for me to go running off – messing about, she called it. I could help for once, she grumbled, to get everything sorted. She had loads to do what with Tim being ill and all the baby's gear to get ready.

"I thought Gran was coming," I told her.

"She rang up to say she couldn't come for another fortnight yet as your grandad wasn't very well. I really ought to go and see *him* but the car drive would be too much for me right now. But you can stay in and help. It's been very tiring nursing Tim. He was really ill and cross."

So are you, I thought, but it didn't do to say it with Mum in a mood. I cleaned and tidied, did some

cooking, walked the dogs.

"Now don't go too far with them, mind. I don't want you getting lost. You're so dreamy these days. No, I *definitely* don't want you going to that tower! I'm not keen on it at all. Who knows who might be wandering round there? Besides, you can read to Tim. His eyes are still hurting

as they do with measles. He can't read much or watch television. Stay at home and *help*!"

I said 'Help!' too, but inside where she couldn't hear, as I didn't want to get my head snapped off. Perhaps Big John would come to the Tower with me sometime, but the Stone brothers told me he'd gone over to the other side of the moor with his dad for a few days. Still, at least Chris and his brother came over to play with Tim, who was out of quarantine now.

With Mrs Cotter back at school, the work got harder. Inspectors were coming, she said, to see how we were getting on. Life was tough again. I remembered that wicked afternoon in the woods with Mrs Biddulph, the best day of school ever, we'd called it, and we'd remember it for always.

But it was gone and we'd said goodbye to Mrs Biddulph. I hadn't liked her at first, but now she seemed like a fairy godmother compared with Mrs Cotter and my mum, who was determined to keep me down.

"Nose to the grindstone, that's what they used to say," shouted Mum, though I noticed she didn't go on at Tim as much.

"He's not well yet," she answered, when I pointed this out.

One morning I took her a cup of tea in bed, tripped and poured it all over her. She shouted at me horribly, and I said, "Mum, why are you so nasty to me these days? I'm doing my best. But there's a lot of homework and a lot of housework and I get—" I couldn't go on. Then I cried, "I wish Dad would come home!"

"So do I," Mum cried. "I'm sorry, Widget. Sorry I was horrible."

She put her arms around me and we both cried. She was soaking with tea and it felt awful, but I felt better. That night Dad phoned us, but he couldn't come home yet, he said.

Next day Mum came out in spots. She'd got measles.

Chapter Eleven

THERE MAY BE TROUBLE AHEAD

The doctor arrived. "She's quite ill," he said to me and Tim, as if we were grown-ups.

"You'd better stay at home to look after her today till I can fix something up. She *may* have to go into hospital. Now, keep the blinds drawn as the light will hurt her eyes. Give her cool drinks. Do you know anyone who can come?"

"My aunt Dinah's gone to America and Gran can't come 'cos Grandad's ill. There's only me. And Tim."

"Hmph. Tim'd best go to school. I'll come

back later. Don't worry now. Just keep her comfortable. I'll see if I can get someone to come and help.

Mum was asleep as she hadn't slept at all the night before. Nor me as I'd gone into bed with her. I got Tim off, fed the animals, put them in their run in the garden. I couldn't watch television. Life was *grim*.

And I was scared. Scared stiff. Suppose she died? People did die. Suppose *she* did. Whatever would we do? How I wished Dad would come. How I wished anyone would come. I'd never felt so lonely in all my life.

Sitting there with her, I tried to imagine the Tower with Lady Nest and Lord Tarquin and the knights and ladies on the lawn, but it wouldn't come. All I could see was Mum in bed, flushed and sweaty and ill.

There was a gentle knock on the door and in walked – what a surprise – Mrs Biddulph. I flung myself on her and howled.

"There! Shhh! She'll be OK. The doctor's sent me to look after her. I did a bit of nursing before I took to teaching, you know. Tried everything in me time. Come on. Cheer up. She'll be fine. I'll get you something to eat. Bet you're starving."

I was, though I hadn't known it. After a bit I fell asleep 'cos I'd been up the night before with Mum. I woke up at last to find I was in bed. Mrs Biddulph had put me there with Hanna and Frizzy all in a heap on my patchwork quilt.

Mum was taken into hospital and put in a ward by herself so that other patients wouldn't catch the measle bug.

People came. Mr Stone, lots of people, but best of all Gran.

"Grandad was fit enough to look after himself," she said. "I'd rather look after you. He keeps telling me off," she whispered.

"Can we visit her? When can we visit her?"

"We'll have to see what the doctor says."

But the doctor made me angry. He said

Tim could visit because he'd had the measles and was now immune. But I hadn't, so I couldn't.

"So am I!" I cried. "I'm immune. I shan't catch measles, I know!"

But nobody took any notice of me. When Gran and Tim went inside, I was left in the car cuddling the dogs. I wanted to know how she looked and how she was. They told me she was comfortable and OK but she longed to see Dad.

I wasn't satisfied. Perhaps they were trying to spare me. And what about the baby? I'd heard that measles could damage unborn babies. I worried and fretted inside.

"Stop sulking," Tim said.

"I'm not sulking. I'm worried. Besides, it's not fair."

"Yes, it is. You were boasty and stuck up when you *didn't* get the measles. Well, now it's my turn."

I kicked him. Gran told me off and I burst out crying.

"I do wish Dad was here."

"He probably wouldn't be able to see her."

"Did he have measles when he was a little boy?"

"Yes, he did. Spots everywhere," Gran said.

"So he *could* see her. There."

A plan was forming in my mind.

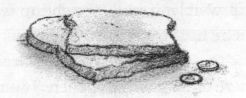

Chapter Twelve

TO THE TOWER

"I'll be OK on my own. Honest."

"Are you sure? I don't like leaving you." Gran's face was worried. "It's all a bit much," she sighed.

"Look – I've got the dogs. I don't want to sit and wait in the car. It's so boring. Here – well, I can lock the doors and if anyone comes I won't answer it and they'll think I've gone with you."

"Well, we'll be quick."

"No, stay as long as Mum wants you and send love and kisses from me."

At last they left. I thought they'd never go, Gran still worrying and wondering was she doing the right thing. I knew she was.

Alone at last, I put on the dogs' leads and slipped out of the back door. They were very quiet as if they knew. We checked Frizzy's puppies. Fine. Getting big now. Off we went, silent and determined. After a bit Death's-head joined us, very subdued for him, as if he knew he couldn't yelp and jump up as usual. I was pleased. Death's-head is so big and ugly he makes you feel safe. Frizzy didn't even squeak.

Off we ran at a steady pace through the fields and the cows to the outskirts of Rushford wood, followed the track leading round it until – I knew the right place this time – we came to the grey granite pillars. The afternoon was clear and still and warm. It was as if we were being welcomed. All my worries gone, I felt happy.

After all, I was going to the Tower. My Tower. Nest's Tower. The Wishing Tower.

★

I couldn't believe it. The wood had turned blue. For the bluebells had blossomed and a misty sea rose before us into the trees. The path wound on and on through the flowers. I let the dogs off the lead; they bounded ahead, tails wagging like crazy. On and on, up and up – the broken-arm-and-hand branch pointed the way. Nothing lay in our path. Nothing to stop us. No brambles. No nettles. Only flowers.

A turn in the path. Almost there. A space opened out, silver birch trees shining white all around; flowers and blossom everywhere, then the lawn of blue-green grass and on the other side of the lawn stood the Tower, its archway inviting me to enter. All was totally still and quiet – the setting sun golden through the tops of the trees.

I felt in my pocket for the silver coins (one for me, one for Tim) and the little bag of bread.

I stopped still. From under the archway appeared an old man; long hair, long grey beard, battered hat on head, long tattered coat with pockets hanging outside, trousers tied with string, toes poking through ancient plimsolls.

We stood still and looked at each other. Pictures of fear swirled through my mind; monsters, ghosts, ghouls, children seized and murdered, terror... But the dogs ran round him, sniffing. Death's-head leapt up to lick his face. Even Frizzy wasn't scared. She lay down at his awful feet.

Besides, I couldn't go back now.

"I've come to wish," I said. "My mother's very ill. I want my dad to come home."

"Yes," he mumbled.

I went nearer. Red Hanna came and walked beside me – she reached up and licked my hand.

"It's my home," he said. I could hear him clearly now.

"I live here. It's my home," he repeated.

I remembered the smelly heap of rubbish in the corner of the room.

"I thought lords and ladies lived here," I whispered sadly.

"No. Only me."

I stood hopelessly lost. Then all his

wrinkles lifted. He broke into a smile.

"But the wishes still come true," he said, "for those who come. Make your wish. Don't be afraid."

The dogs stood round me as I put the silver coin and the bread just inside the archway. The tramp moved away.

"Can I have a bit of the bread and one of the coins?" he asked.

"But they're for Tim—" I said and stopped. "No, it doesn't matter. You have them."

He took a coin and some bread and disappeared inside. I buried the rest under the stones as John had showed me, and walked slowly across the lawn. Then, reaching the path and trees, we pelted down the hill as fast as the wind till we reached Goosey Farm.

When we burst into the kitchen Dad was there cooking a huge fry-up.

"Gosh, I'm starving!" he laughed as I ran to him.

Chapter Thirteen

MAGIC IS REAL

Everyone came: Dad on leave, Mum spotless now, Gran, Grandad, Aunt Dinah back with boyfriend Fred (again!), all the children and teachers from school, Mr Stone and people from the neighbouring farms.

And I was godmother. ME.

Godmother to James Thomas.

I was sorry at first he wasn't a girl, but he's OK. Quite neat. And I'll be *boss*, anyway.

We had a scrumptious party with wicked grub. I looked for John and found him sitting outside on a wall. There was something I wanted to ask.

"Did you see that old tramp slipping away when we came out of church?"

"Yup."

"You know everybody round here."

"Yup."

"Who is he?"

"'E won't 'arm you, Widget."

"I know that. But who is he?"

"Oh 'e's old Arthur Merlyn."

"Did you say Merlyn?"

"Yup. Old name roundabouts 'ere, y'know."

"Widget..." my dad was calling me. "...come and have your photo taken. Holding the baby, I think."

Merlyn. Merlin. My head whizzed.

"Widget. Come on."

"OK. Coming!"

Merlin, I'd think about it later, later.

Epilogue

In *Dog's Journey* I told you about Mum's painting of Russet that hangs above the mantelpiece. On the wall opposite is another. It shows a little grey tower in the middle of a wood. In the corner is written *"Widget's Wishing Tower*, by Madeleine Sutton".

Widget Sutton
1998